W9-BKD-242

MINIONS

Dracula's Last Birthday

By Lucy Rosen
Illustrated by Ed Miller

LB kids

Minions © 2015 Universal Studios. Minions is a trademark and copyright of Universal Studios. Licensed by Universal Studios Licensing LLC. All rights reserved. • In accordance with the U.S. Copyright Act of 1976, the scanning, uploading, and electronic sharing of any part of this book without the permission of the publisher is unlawful piracy and theft of the author's intellectual property. If you would like to use material from the book (other than for review purposes), prior written permission must be obtained by contacting the publisher at permissions@hbgusa.com. Thank you for your support of the author's rights. • Little, Brown and Company • Hachette Book Group • 1290 Avenue of the Americas, New York, NY 10104 • Visit us at lb-kids.com • LB kids is an imprint of Little, Brown and Company. The LB kids name and logo are trademarks of Hachette Book Group, Inc. • The publisher is not responsible for websites (or their content) that are not owned by the publisher. • First Edition: July 2015 • Library of Congress Control Number: 2015930748 • ISBN 978-0-316-29998-5 • 10 9 8 7 6 5 4 3 2 1 • CW • minionsmovie.com

Printed in the United States of America

Minions have roamed the earth since the beginning of time. Before there was Gru, before there were evil gadgets to invent, before there were super villains who wanted to take over the world…there were Minions.

Ever since the very first Minion crawled out of the ocean and onto dry land, these little yellow creatures have been searching for one thing: the most terrible, wicked, despicable master they could find.

The Minions lived to serve.
They had no trouble tracking
down the biggest, baddest
dinosaur…

…or helping a wicked pharaoh
erect a pyramid.

But even though they just wanted to help, something always went wrong.

Whenever disaster struck, the Minions kept moving. One day, they came across a dark stone castle. It looked creepy, creaky, and cold. It was perfect! The Minions couldn't wait to meet whoever lived there.

The Minions pushed open the front door and peeked inside. Out of nowhere, bats came flying toward them! "Oh, la no! Stopa, stopa!" they cried, trying to get away from the bat attack. The Minions tumbled into dusty cobwebs. They jumped into sticky cauldrons. They hid behind heavy, dirty curtains.

When the bats finally left, the Minions came out of their hiding spots and looked around. At the end of the long, dark hallway was a spooky wooden coffin. "Oooooh," they said.

One of the Minions walked up to the coffin. He knocked on the lid. It burst wide open. Dracula was inside!

"Velcome to my castle!" the evil vampire bellowed.

"Si, si, si!" cried the Minions. They couldn't believe it. They had found their new master!

"Big boss! Big boss! Big boss!" they cheered.

BIG BOSS!

The Minions got right to work trying to help Dracula however they could. First, they decided to clean up the castle. Carl and Mike took turns sweeping the cobwebs.

"Me do it," Carl said.

"No, me, me do it," Mike replied.

"Speta, me la do it," Carl insisted.

"Me!" said Mike.

"Me!" said Carl.

Soon enough, the two Minions were tussling down the hallway. They bounced and rolled and rumbled all around, until they got tangled up in an enormous web!

Next, the Minions replaced all of Dracula's melted candles. One by one, they removed the old wax. They carefully polished each candlestick. They gently put in fresh new candles.

Then they lit them all with a torch.

Finally, at the end of every day, the Minions helped Dracula get ready to go to sleep. They hung up his cape, fluffed his itchy pillow, and reminded him to always brush his fangs before bedtime.

"Scusa, big boss? Floss-floss?" they said.

Dental Floss

Over time, Dracula came to rely on the Minions and think of them as his friends. He even let them in on a secret.

"Tomorrow vill be my three-hundred-und-fifty-seventh birthday!" he said proudly.

The Minions were excited. They wanted to throw their evil boss an evil party to celebrate his many years of evildoing. But they didn't have much time.

Kevin made a list of all the things they'd need to do: Bake a cake. Make drinks. Find a great gift…

Dave and Paul got started on the cake. They mixed together eggs, flour, strawberries, and sugar. "Yum, yum," they said.

Chuck and Norbert made punch in one of Dracula's cauldrons. They put ice cream and fresh fruit in the juice. Delicious!

Finding the right gift was the hardest part. What does a Minion get for the villain who has it all? The Minions put their heads together until they thought of the perfect present: a portrait of Dracula with all his yellow friends by his side.

They got to work painting their masterpiece.

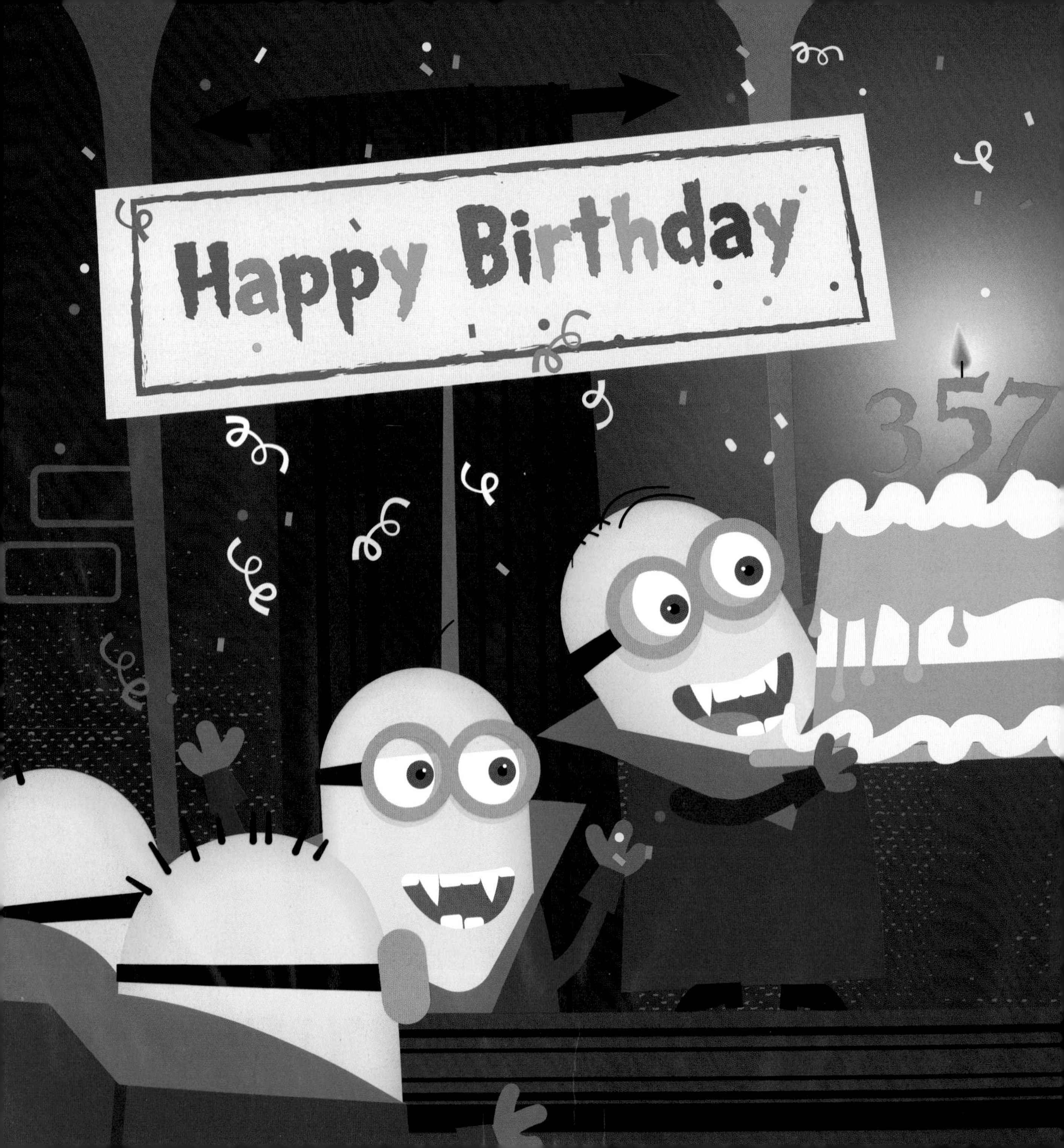
Happy Birthday
357

Finally, it was time! The big day had arrived. Dave and Paul led Dracula to the ballroom, where the party was just getting started.

"Surprise!" the Minions yelled.

"Ah, how vonderful!" Dracula cackled as he sipped from his goblet of fruit punch.

"Big boss, big cake," said Kevin. He opened the door to reveal Minions carrying a strawberries-and-cream cake.

Dracula took a deep breath and blew out the candles.

They were about to give Dracula his present when Norbert realized it was too dark to see. They had gone to a lot of trouble making it perfect, and he wanted to make sure their boss would enjoy it.

"Le idea!" Kevin said.

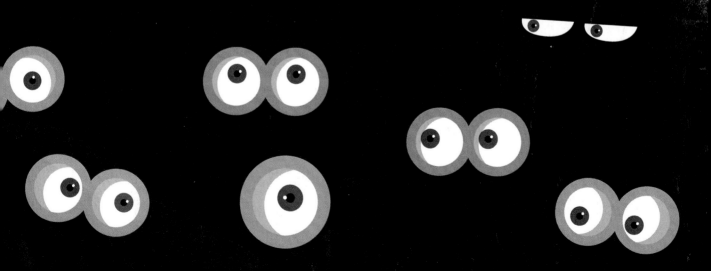

The Minions grabbed the curtains and pulled them apart. Sunlight poured in and onto their painting.

"Paratu, big boss!" the Minions cooed, admiring their work of art.

Dracula didn't reply.

"Big boss?" they said.

Dracula did not say a word.

The Minions turned around.

Where Dracula had been sitting, there was now a big pile of ashes. The Minions forgot about the vampire's biggest weakness: sunlight!

"Uh, no," said Stuart, slapping his forehead. "Not again."

Another evil boss,
another Minion accident.
The little yellow creatures
sighed and moved on.

Soon, they found
another perfect
despicable master in
a French captain. At
least—that is—until
they messed up again.

OOPS!

TM & © Universal Studios